THE
STONE LION

To Ethel and "Big Al" Lerche, with love
—A.S.

Library of Congress Cataloging-in-Publication Data.
Schroeder, Alan.   The stone lion / Alan Schroeder ; pictures by Todd L. W. Doney. — 1st ed.
    p.   cm.   Summary: Two Tibetan brothers are rewarded appropriately by a stone lion,
one for his generosity and one for his greed.
ISBN 0-684-19578-X
[1. Folklore—Tibet.]   I. Doney, Todd, ill.   II. Title.   PZ8. 1. S37St   1994
398. 21—dc20   [E]   92-38257

THE STONE LION

Alan Schroeder

Pictures by Todd L. W. Doney

CHARLES SCRIBNER'S SONS · NEW YORK
Maxwell Macmillan Canada · Toronto
Maxwell Macmillan International
New York · Oxford · Singapore · Sydney

Once upon a time, in the barren hills of Tibet, there lived a widow named Tsomo and her two sons, Jarlo and Drashi. Jarlo, the elder, was the village goldsmith. He was a cold and greedy merchant who cheated his customers and lied about the quality of his wares.

Drashi, on the other hand, was extremely good-hearted. He was never too busy to fill the water *kang* for a neighbor or help his mother pound barley at the bread trough.

When Drashi was ten, Tsomo took him aside and said to him, "You are old enough now to become an apprentice to your brother. Pay attention, and do whatever he tells you."

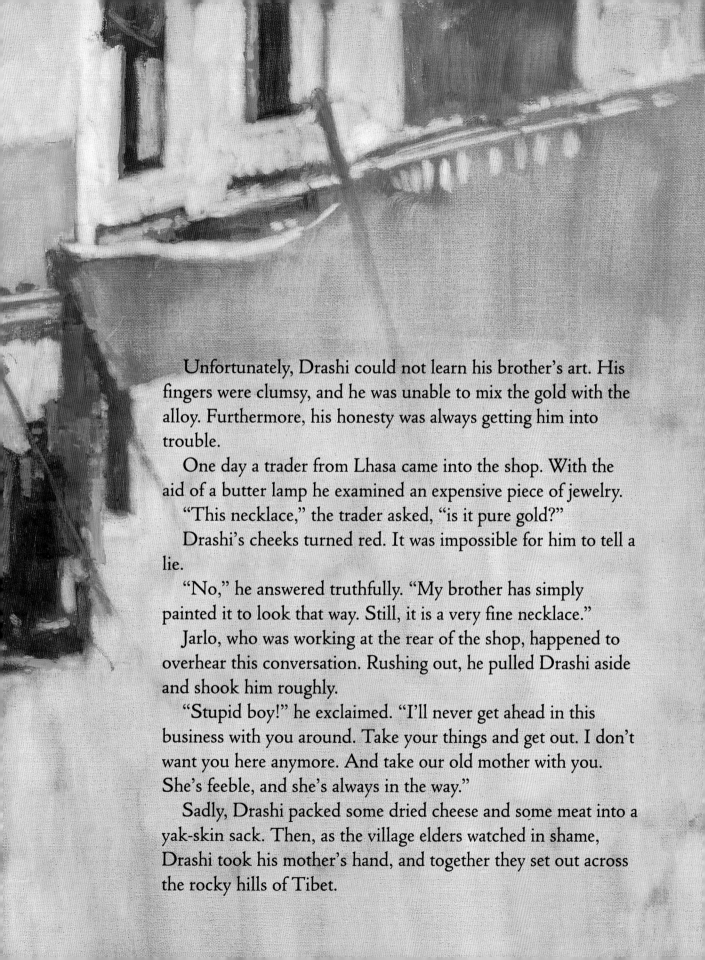

Unfortunately, Drashi could not learn his brother's art. His fingers were clumsy, and he was unable to mix the gold with the alloy. Furthermore, his honesty was always getting him into trouble.

One day a trader from Lhasa came into the shop. With the aid of a butter lamp he examined an expensive piece of jewelry.

"This necklace," the trader asked, "is it pure gold?"

Drashi's cheeks turned red. It was impossible for him to tell a lie.

"No," he answered truthfully. "My brother has simply painted it to look that way. Still, it is a very fine necklace."

Jarlo, who was working at the rear of the shop, happened to overhear this conversation. Rushing out, he pulled Drashi aside and shook him roughly.

"Stupid boy!" he exclaimed. "I'll never get ahead in this business with you around. Take your things and get out. I don't want you here anymore. And take our old mother with you. She's feeble, and she's always in the way."

Sadly, Drashi packed some dried cheese and some meat into a yak-skin sack. Then, as the village elders watched in shame, Drashi took his mother's hand, and together they set out across the rocky hills of Tibet.

After passing through numerous valleys they came to the foot of a very large mountain. Exhausted, Drashi's mother set down her pack.

"Son," she said, "I cannot climb any higher. We will have to make our home here, at the base of this mountain. Go and dig up a few roots, and collect some deadwood for a fire. But, mind, do not cut the branches of any living tree, or you will anger the Guardian of the Mountain, and he will send down a *yeti* to eat us during the night."

Drashi did as he was told, collecting only the branches and leaves that lay upon the ground. Over a three-stone campfire, his mother, Tsomo, cooked a pot of rice and boiled some broth, and in this way, they spent their first lonely night at the base of the mountain.

Many days passed. Not far from where they had camped, Drashi and his mother came across an old hut built of stone and mud. Nearby there was a swift-running stream, and every morning, at sunrise, Drashi plunged his hands into the freezing water, trying to catch a squirming fish. His mother, meanwhile, collected roots and prepared yogurt and tea for the afternoon meal.

At night it was bitterly cold on the mountain, but inside the hut, next to the fire, Drashi felt safe and warm. Once a week he watched his mother patiently braid her hair into one hundred and eight strands. In Tibet this was a holy number, and to keep the braids in place, Tsomo would smear her hair with yak butter. All the while she would tell Drashi stories about her girlhood in the far-off city of Lhasa. Other times, when the wind came howling down the mountain, she would warn Drashi about the evil spirits that haunted the hills of Tibet.

"That is why we burn juniper twigs," she told him. "To scare off those spirits that would otherwise do us harm."

Bit by bit, Drashi could feel himself growing sleepy. He rested his head in his mother's lap and closed his eyes. Tsomo went on with her task, silently counting her braids and repeating her prayers under her breath. An hour later, when she had finished, she glanced down. Drashi was fast asleep.

Half a year passed. Their life on the mountain became more difficult. Every now and then the stream ran dry; the roof of their hut leaked when it rained; and each morning, Drashi had to climb higher and higher to find enough deadwood to keep the campfire burning.

One afternoon he found himself at the very top of the mountain. There, to his surprise, he discovered a large, fierce-looking lion carved entirely out of stone.

"You must be the Guardian of the Mountain," said Drashi. "My mother has told me about you." And reaching into his sack, he took out his prayer wheel. He also took out two candles, which he lit and placed upon the ground. At that moment the fearsome lion opened his mouth and began to speak.

"Who are you," he demanded, "and what are you doing up here, where few ever dare to come?"

Drashi, naturally, was frightened. He wondered if the lion was going to eat him.

"I am collecting wood," he managed to say, his eyes respectfully fixed upon the ground.

"There are plenty of trees farther down the mountain," growled the lion. "Go away, and leave me alone."

Drashi lifted his gaze. The lion's words seemed to give him courage.

"But those trees are still growing," he replied. "I'm looking for dead branches only. My mother has told me that the roots of the trees hold the soil together, and this keeps the streams and the rivers from overflowing. Also, the trees on this mountain are beautiful and many animals live in their branches. My mother says that if I were to cut down one living tree, it would only be a matter of time before I would cut them all down, and that would ruin the mountain."

The lion seemed pleased to hear this.

"You are a good boy," he growled softly. "Come closer, and hang your bucket under my chin." Sternly, the lion watched the boy's every move. "Now, with your right hand, begin rubbing my mane. Whatever falls into the bucket is yours to keep. But you must warn me when the bucket is nearly full. Do not try to trick me, or you will be punished for your greed."

Gently, Drashi began stroking the lion's mane. To his amazement a sparkling stream of gold and silver coins started pouring from the lion's jaws. It was a glorious sight to behold, like a swift river glinting in the sunlight. When the bucket was nearly full, Drashi stopped rubbing the lion's mane, and at once the stream of coins dried up.

"Now go," said the lion, "and do not return. May your life be long and prosperous."

Drashi knelt to express his thanks, but at that instant the lion became stone again, his mouth frozen as though it had never opened.

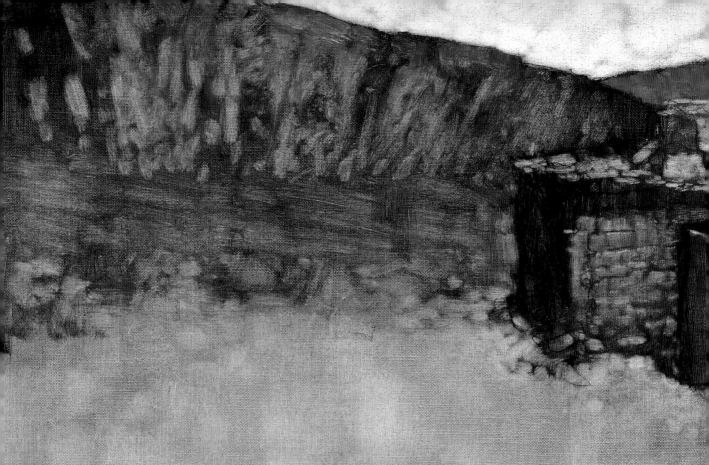

Quickly Drashi blew out the candles and ran down the mountain, straight to his mother's hut. Tsomo was near the river, setting out a bamboo snare. When she saw the heavy bucket of gold and silver coins, she clapped her hands in delight.

"Our troubles are over!" she cried, tears of happiness flowing down her weathered cheeks. "Come, son, we'll light a candle to Vaishravana, the god of wealth, for he has been very good to us and we must thank him properly."

With their new-found fortune, Drashi and his mother were able to buy plenty of food, acres of rich pastureland, and hundreds of wool-bearing sheep. Their life was comfortable and happy, and because they traded fairly and took advantage of no one, they were respected throughout the region.

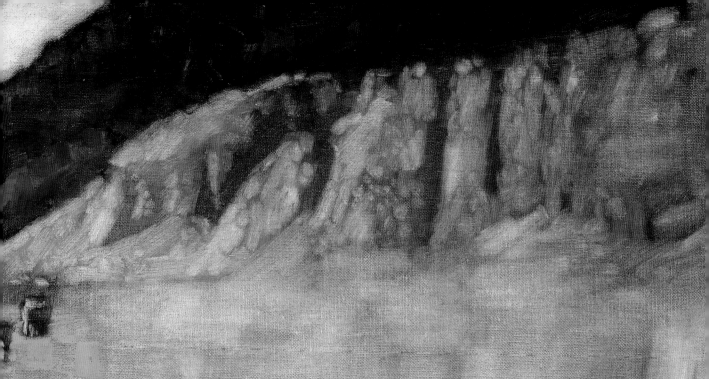

Before long, word of their prosperity reached the bustling village where Drashi and his mother used to live. At first Jarlo, the crafty goldsmith, could not believe his ears.

"How did my brother become so wealthy?" he asked his wife, Ani. "When I sent him away he had nothing, not even his wits, and now, in less than a year's time, he has become one of the largest landowners in Tibet. Come, we'll visit him, and find out his secret."

And packing their things into a sturdy yak-skin sack, they set out across the windswept mountains and valleys.

When Jarlo reached his brother's large and comfortable home at the base of the mountain, he pretended to be very surprised.

"Mother," he said, fingering the handsome necklace that hung around Tsomo's neck, "you have everything you could possibly want. How on earth did you do it? You started out with practically nothing. Come, old woman, you can tell me. I'm your son."

But Tsomo refused to say. She knew that Jarlo was not to be trusted.

Annoyed, the goldsmith turned to his younger brother.

"I know you, Drashi. You can't tell a lie. Where did your fortune come from?"

And in this way Jarlo learned about the bountiful stone lion at the top of the mountain. That evening, before going to bed, he had a hushed conversation with his wife.

"Tomorrow we're going up there," he whispered. "We mustn't forget to bring a bucket and a rope. If we can, we'll drag the lion home and force him to spit out gold day and night for the next ten years. I'm surprised my stupid brother hasn't thought of that already."

The next morning, at dawn, Jarlo and his wife slipped out of the house and began climbing the steep mountain. After many tiring hours they reached the windswept peak. There, in a lonely spot, they discovered the Guardian of the Mountain sitting on his stone pedestal.

"Wake up, lion!" commanded Jarlo, lighting two candles he had stolen from his brother's house.

The lion opened his eyes.

"Who are you," he growled, "and what are you doing up here, where few men dare to tread?"

"We're looking for firewood," answered Jarlo, holding up an ax.

"There are plenty of trees farther down the mountain," said the lion.

"Oh, we've already chopped them down. The mountainside is bare. That's why we've come all the way up here, to look for more."

The lion's eyes hardened.

"Come closer," he growled, "and hang your bucket under my chin."

Jarlo quickly obeyed, thinking all the while of the fortune that would soon be his. Dark clouds, in the meantime, were beginning to form above the mountain.

"Now, with your right hand, begin rubbing my mane," said the lion. "Whatever falls into the bucket is yours to keep. But you must warn me when the bucket is nearly full. Do not try to trick me, or you will be punished for your greed. Do you understand?"

"Yes, yes," said Jarlo impatiently. "Let's get started."

With short, jerky motions he began stroking the lion's mane, and just as he expected, a glorious stream of gold and silver coins began pouring from the lion's jaws. Jarlo did not notice that the clouds were growing darker and that an icy blast of wind seemed to be coming from the lion's mouth. His eyes were fixed greedily on the sparkling pile of money, which had nearly reached the top of the bucket.

"Perhaps we should warn the lion now," his wife whispered, but Jarlo pushed her aside and, seizing the bucket, he gave it a good shake, in order to make room for more money. This caused several of the coins to slide over the edge and tumble to the ground. Instantly the gold and silver stream dried up.

"What is it, what's wrong?" cried Jarlo, highly alarmed.

"Ah," said the lion in a raspy voice, "the biggest coin of all is stuck in my throat. Perhaps you can pull it out, and we'll continue where we left off."

Without even thinking, Jarlo thrust his forearm eagerly into the lion's mouth. *Snap!* In an instant the stony jaws came down, trapping Jarlo in their grip.

For a moment the goldsmith thought it was a joke, but when he realized what had happened, a terrible fear clutched his heart. Frantically he began pulling and tugging, but to no avail.

"Help me!" he screamed. Ani tried jumping on the lion's tail, but the beast did not move, and the gold and silver coins, she saw, had turned to ashes.

Then the full fury of the storm broke above their heads. Jarlo could hardly make himself heard above the piercing howl of the wind.

"Go back down the mountain," he shouted to his wife, "and fetch me a blanket. And, whatever you do, don't shame me by telling my family what has happened. No one must know."

Much later that evening, after the storm had calmed, Ani returned, bringing with her two blankets and a small store of food. She also brought a ceremonial scarf, to show respect for the lion. But the stone beast remained silent, his eyes staring straight ahead.

That night, and for many nights thereafter, Jarlo lived at the top of the mountain. One day Ani came to him, her face streaked with tears. "I have sold everything," she said. "The shop, our home, even our clothing—it is all gone. We have nothing left."

Jarlo's eyes were moist. He, too, had been weeping.

"I am deeply sorry," he said, "for what has happened. My brother deserved the fortune he received, and I have been a fool. I never should have tried to cheat the stone lion."

At this the lion's jaws sprang open, and from his throat there issued a tremendous laugh that shook the entire mountain range.

"Run!" Ani cried, but Jarlo had already pulled out his arm and was flying down the mountainside as fast as his feet could carry him.

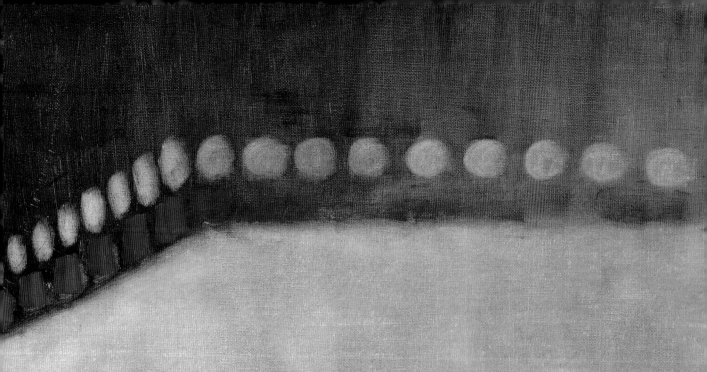

He fled straight to his brother's house, and, throwing himself on the doorstep, he begged forgiveness for his selfish behavior.

Drashi not only forgave his elder brother, but presented him with the last of the coins he had received from the stone lion. Jarlo used this money to buy himself a tiny cottage far, far away. And though he often came to visit his mother and brother, never again did he go anywhere near the Guardian of the Mountain.

Many years later, when he was an old man, Drashi climbed to the top of the mountain. He wanted to visit his friend the lion once more, to thank him for the good things he had received in life. He searched and searched, but the stone lion had long ago crumbled to dust—had become one with the rocky soil of Tibet.

The old pedestal, however, was still there, and, bending down, Drashi said a quiet prayer of thanks. Then, with peace in his heart, he grasped his walking stick and began the long journey home.